REBELS
.102300.862118.000012
GHOST SHIP
001036.10
STAR WARS
Rebel
001000
11
10
010

REBELS
001036,102900,862118,000012
GHOST SHIP
STAR WARS
001000 II IO

STAR WARS REBELS™

CHOPPER
SAVES THE DAY

Based on the episode "The Machine in the *Ghost*,"
written by Greg Weisman

Adapted by Elizabeth Schaefer

© & ™ 2014 Lucasfilm Ltd.

Published by Disney • Lucasfilm Press, an imprint of Disney Book Group. No part of this book may be reproduced or transmitted in any form or by any means, electronic or mechanical, including photocopying, recording, or by any information storage and retrieval system, without written permission from the publisher. For information address Disney • Lucasfilm Press, 1101 Flower Street, Glendale, California 91201.

Printed in China

First Edition, December 2014
1 3 5 7 9 10 8 6 4 2

ISBN 978-1-4847-2604-4
T425-2382-5-14356

Visit the official *Star Wars* website at: www.starwars.com
This book was printed on paper created from a sustainable source.

DisNep
LUCASFILM
P R E S S

Los Angeles • New York

Hera Syndulla gripped the controls of her ship, the *Ghost*. As pilot of the rebel craft, she had taken on plenty of Imperial TIE fighters before. On a good day, Hera could outmaneuver almost any ship. But Hera was not having a good day.

As four TIE fighters opened fire on the *Ghost*, she knew she needed help.

"Kanan, we have a small situation here," Hera called to her crewmate as the TIE fighters closed in on them. "If you'd care to blast one of these TIEs out of the galaxy, I don't think anyone would object."

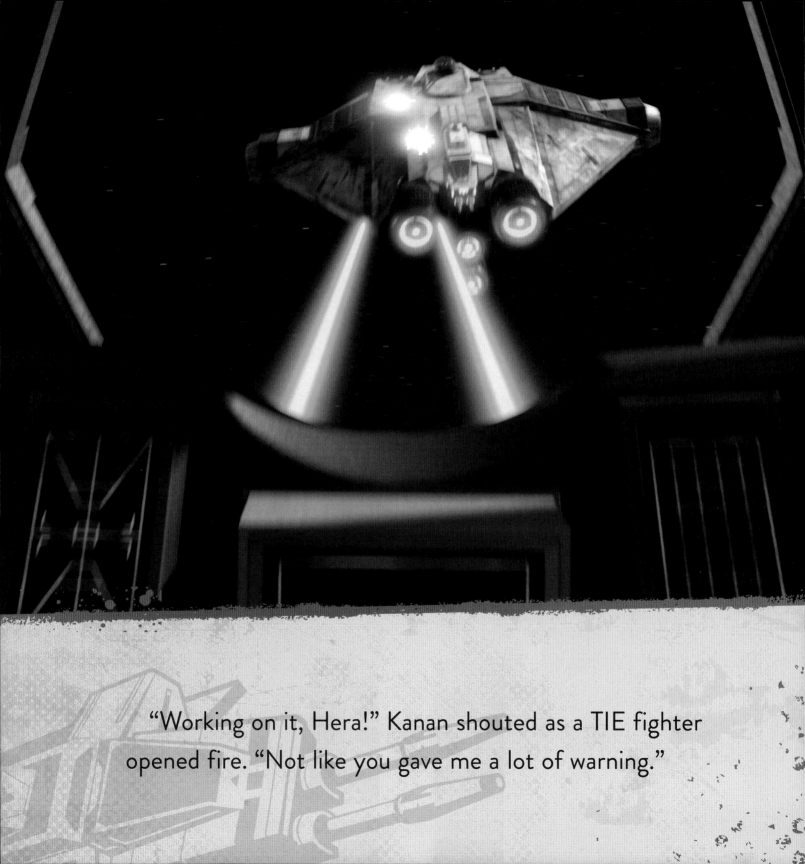

"Working on it, Hera!" Kanan shouted as a TIE fighter opened fire. "Not like you gave me a lot of warning."

"As I recall, raiding an Imperial supply convoy was your plan," Hera replied through the ship's communication link.

That stumped Kanan. "Well, it made sense at the time!"

Kanan climbed the ladder to the ship's gun turret and grabbed the controls. Within moments he had shot down one of the TIE fighters! But there were still three ships left, and they were not going down without a fight.

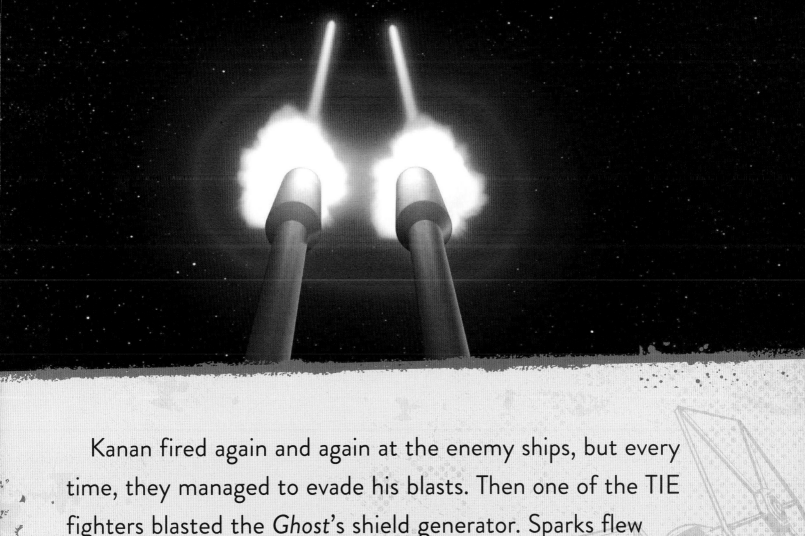

Kanan fired again and again at the enemy ships, but every time, they managed to evade his blasts. Then one of the TIE fighters blasted the *Ghost*'s shield generator. Sparks flew everywhere as the rebel ship shook from the impact.

"Shields down!" Hera groaned as the display in front of her began beeping wildly. But Hera stayed calm. She called out to the ship's astromech droid: "Chopper, fix them!"

Chopper was a bit grouchy sometimes, but there was no other droid Hera would rather have in a tight spot.

Chopper heard Hera's request and beeped in irritation. Of course he was going to fix the ship's shields. Hera didn't need to remind him to save all their lives. Again.

Hera didn't register Chopper's annoyance. She was a little busy dodging the TIE fighters. "Kanan, what part of 'blast them' did you not understand?" she joked into the ship's intercom. "Kanan, do you read?" But there was no answer.

"Internal comm is out. Chopper, go back to comm control and fix it," Hera yelled to the droid.

Chopper beeped unhappily. He had just started repairing the shields!

"I know you're fixing the shields," Hera replied, "but I need comm operational to coordinate our attack."

WHACK! Chopper banged his head against the shield control console in frustration. Then he headed down inside the ship to the gun turret ladder.

"And while you're back there, tell Kanan to please hit something!" Hera called after the droid.

Chopper grumbled to himself; then he beeped Hera's instructions up to Kanan.

"I'm a little busy, Chop," Kanan said as he blasted one of the TIE fighters out of the sky. "Wait, what are you doing back here? Shouldn't you be fixing the shields?"

Chopper beeped that Hera had sent him to fix the comm.

"I don't need to talk to Captain Hera right now," Kanan said, frustrated. "Get back up there and fix the shields!"

Chopper was not amused. Rolling back and forth between the shields and the intercom wasn't helping anyone, least of all Chopper.

As Chopper dutifully began moving toward the cockpit, Kanan shouted after him: "Oh, yeah. And when you see Hera, tell her to fly better!"

When Chopper reached the cockpit, he took a little too much joy in telling Hera to "fly better."

"Oh, he said that, did he?" Hera asked with a tight smile. *Well*, Hera thought, *I'll just have to show Kanan a thing or two about shooting down TIE fighters.*

Hera expertly maneuvered the *Ghost* in a swift arc around one of the enemy ships. The Imperial pilot tried to evade her blasts, but Hera quickly fired everything she had at the ship's exhaust vents. The third TIE fighter exploded in a burst of laser fire. "Do I have to do *everything* myself?" Hera asked with a smirk.

Hera leaned back in her chair. "Tell our fearless leader he should be able to handle one lone TIE fighter on his own."

Chopper pretended to beep in agreement. But the droid was done rolling back and forth between the cockpit and the gun turret. He was an astromech droid, not an answering machine!

Chopper knew it was time to take matters into his own mechanical hands. He left the cockpit and wheeled quickly past Kanan in the gun turret.

The droid interfaced directly with the ship's rear cannon and, with a satisfied beep, fired on the last TIE fighter.

The enemy ship exploded with a *BOOM!* Then everything was still. The *Ghost* had made it through another battle safely.

As Chopper returned to the cockpit, he heard Hera's voice.
"All right, I'll admit it. That was some fine shooting."

Chopper beeped happily to himself as he entered the
cockpit—only to realize that Hera was complimenting Kanan.

Chopper began beeping furiously.

"Just kidding, Chop," Kanan interrupted him hastily.

"We know you got that last one," Hera added. "Good work."

Chopper waved off their praise with his mechanical arm.
But his crewmates' admiration was not very long lived.

"Now get that comm fixed," Kanan told the droid.

"And the shields," Hera added. "Don't forget the shields."

Chopper beep-sighed again. An astromech droid's work
was never done!